Daddy Is My Hero

Dawn Richards ★ Jane Massey

Picture Corgi

DADDY IS MY HERO
A PICTURE CORGI BOOK 978 0 552 56915 6
First published in Great Britain by Picture Corgi,
an imprint of Random House Children's Publishers UK
A Random House Group Company
This edition published 2013

10 9 8 7 6

Penguin Random House is committed to a sustainable future for our business, our readers and our planet.
This book is made from Forest Stewardship Council® certified paper.

MIX
Paper from
responsible sources
FSC® C013123

My daddy
looks quite normal,
no different from
the rest . . .

But my daddy
is a **hero**,

the greatest dad,

the best!

My daddy does
the shopping.

He cooks and
cleans for me.

But if you think that's
all he does, well just
you wait and see . . .

My daddy is a sheriff,

he rides through night and day.

He captures wicked outlaws
and he locks them all away.

My daddy is a knight of old,
he's always on a quest . . .

He battles
greedy dragons
and saves people
in distress.

My daddy runs
a bath for me,
with bubbles
and shampoo.

He helps
me with my
toothbrush . . .

but there's
much more
he can do . . .

My daddy is a captain,
he sails across the sea.

And when I'm caught by pirates, he is there to rescue me.

My dad's a deep-sea diver,
he swims beneath the blue.

He battles with
sea monsters and
finds sunken
treasure too.

My daddy doesn't always win . . .

He isn't always right . . .

Sometimes I get cross
with him, and sometimes
there's a fight . . .

But I KNOW my daddy loves me.
I know he's ALWAYS there.

I know he's there to hug me,
to look after me and care.

My daddy reads me stories,
a new one every night.
But can you guess what happens
when he switches off the light?

My daddy flies a spaceship,
he zooms among the stars.

He scares away the aliens

from Jupiter and Mars.

My daddy is a wizard,
he knows all sorts
of spells . . .

He calms the wild monsters
with the stories that he tells.

My daddy is MY hero,

and if I'm ever sad . . .

He tickles me
and makes me laugh
and stops me
feeling bad.

My daddy looks quite normal,
no different from
the rest . . .

But Daddy is my hero . . .
the greatest dad,
the best!